Empress Dawn

Casey Brandt

Crow's Foot Publishing
Austin, Texas

EMPRESS DAWN

ISBN: 978-1-7325812-0-3
Ebook: 978-1-7325812-1-0

Crow's Foot Publishing
Austin, Texas

To my love and wife, Shannon, for being my reason and inspiration. Thank you for holding back the tides of chaos every single day and helping me find the space to create.

And to my daughter, the toughest cookie I know.

And also to my boys, who will be like a bundle of sticks.

Empress Dawn

ONE

In a dark time on a remote world the princess Dawn walked without her mother's knowledge through a forbidden forest in search of lands of legend. She danced in the love-laden birdsong pouring from the trees, chased the prancing does that protected their young, and followed the blooming flower paths that flowed through dense foliage, until one dew-covered morning when she heard a soft whisper on the wind beckoning her to follow. Half cheerful, half fearful she pulled her violet velvet hood over her copper curls and floated on faint footsteps toward the melodic whispering voice.

Deeper into the woods she pranced along with all kinds of curious creatures, knocking up puffs of golden spore until she caught the scent of wolf and hurried with a giggle along the trail where the whisper led her. Over a bubbling stream, under twisted trees, and into an open glade lined with yellow mushroom. There in its center stood an icy black shadow of a man that froze her in her tracks, wide-eyed and numb. The sable statue stood in stark contrast to the lush green garden. Panic seized her throat as the statue raised a hand of stirring black sand, extended a hardened stone finger, and pointed out beyond to a massive mound rising from the rear of the clearing. At that instant the statue vanished, blown away in a cloud of black smoke, and the whisper was replaced with the unmistakable cries of an infant child that melted her fright and compelled her to find it.

With her first step toward the bawling, she was startled further by the harrowing howl of a lone wolf behind her, who had followed her frolic and now also sought the crying child. Emerging from the tree line like a blade from its sheath came the alpha, accompanied by its pack. They stabbed the air with their snouts searching for the fragrant rosy flesh of the princess. Dawn's tender heart stilled at the realization that she had ventured farther than the woodsman Cano had cleared. Her breath vanished at the sight of the bristling gray furs, scarred faces, and ivory dagger teeth. She suppressed her own dreadful screams with a trembling hand and wondered at the rightness of her mother's wicked warnings. With a deathly numbness she fled into the grass field, where the massive mound now had a narrow sliver opened on its face from which the cries came. She ran to it without looking back, slid sideways between the stone walls, emerged into a near-pitch chamber illuminated only by the sharp slice of light cast through the entrance.

From inside, the infant's crying guided her around tangled vines, mossy lumps, and jutting stone protrusions that were like the innards of a giant earthen carcass. The hazy echoes resounded through the depths of the hypogeum and gradually dizzied her unshielded mind. Amid the dark she found the crying babe. Its warm smooth skin was as pure as her own and its kicking feet tickled her palms. She imagined her mother scolding her for her actions, hesitated a moment, then resolved to save the little life.

She strained to lift the child, which felt as heavy as lead, and in her arms its crying waned, allowing silence to fill the dark void within the mound.

"Oh, precious little one," she whispered and kissed a tear-streaked cheek, tasting an essence of honey. "How did you get here?"

The baby cooed a calm reply in Dawn's arms and tugged at the threaded ribbons of her silk corset. She bore the youngling back into the light and out of the mound's fissure, where she found that the wolf pack had encircled her but kept its distance. The alpha snapped and snarled, but did not approach with the child in Dawn's arms.

The dander of the canines disturbed the baby greatly, which in the light was revealed to be a boy with extraordinary eyes—one sparkling sapphire, one splendid emerald, both bright as stars and lucid as the castle elder's. The boy returned a low growl that shook the alpha to its core and wavered its will, giving it cause to flee the field into the forest with its pack in tow. Dawn sighed with relief, held the boy close as the night began to fall and her paralyzing dread returned. She retreated to the mound and endured the night in a frightened wakefulness that was only eased by the boy's playful prattle.

In the early morning, as the sun crawled into view, the princess cast off her tiredness and bore the baby back through the teeming forest confident yet cautious as she found her way to Cano's cabin. He had just returned with fresh wolf pelts and a peregrine on his shoulder when she blew him a kiss and leaped onto the back of her mare to journey home to her mother's castle like a rock dove returning to its keeper. Her laughter had left her, replaced with regard for the child she hugged tight and also the fear of her mother's interrogation.

At the old gates of the mighty ancient fortress, guards drew down the bridge, raised up the portcullis, and separated for the prince brother who boldly blocked his sister's arrival.

"Where have you been?" he lashed with a voice like a snapping whip. "Mother is not happy. And by the dark gods of Mawveth, what do you have there?"

"This child needs our aid," Dawn said gently while hiding the boy's face under her long bell sleeve. Her eyes were cool and calm. They chilled the prince's anger. "Mother can be patient. Send for the elder's apothecary nourishment."

The prince wrinkled his face and laughed at his sister's absurdity. "Let me see this child you toy with. Since you will not tell from where it came, I'll read it for myself."

"Where *he* came. And I found him in the woods." She stepped back, avoiding his reach.

"The woods you are not permitted to visit or speak of," the prince scolded with a sideways stare. "Mother will hear of this, you will be punished for certain," he said with a smile and beaming eyes full of excitement. "And your baby will be thrown from the spire. You there," the prince waved a ringed hand to his guard, "escort my sister to the queen."

In the court chamber of the impenetrable keep sat the Nightmare Queen on her stiletto throne. Dark metal pikes rose behind her back like sharpened spider's legs while she sat upright in her royal midnight-purple gown with its floral ornaments and decorative beads. Hung over her heart was a knotted cross of ashen metal, twisted around a matte-black orb. An indigo ruff hid her neck. A violet veil covered her vile eyes, which were affixed to a porcelain face with shadowy features. She sat motionless, her breath imperceptible.

"Why have you ignored my warning, Daughter?" she hissed like a venomous serpent with glossy, distant eyes.

"Mother, I know what you will say," Dawn said over the senseless banter of the baby. "So I will spare you the trouble: the baby was alone and dying. I had to take him to save his life."

"Save his life," the queen repeated. "Bring him close; perhaps he will be fit for offering to Mawveth." She seethed under her veil, leaned forward to see further.

Dawn obeyed with a wrenching gut and approached her queen mother.

The doors opened behind them, and the elder strode into the room followed by the prince brother. The elder's red robes swayed as he stepped. His olive trousers, embroidered with gold thread, heralded his venerated intellect. A long gray beard grew from his old chin. His textured skin was wrinkled like unclean parchment.

"Gnostro," the queen uttered. "My daughter entered the forbidden wood and returned with this child. What say you of its nature?"

"Sovereign majesty, allow me," he said, then saluted the matriarch and turned to Dawn who recoiled from his advance. "Please, my lady, allow my inspection."

"You may inspect this child from where you stand," Dawn retorted with a forceful glare that stayed the elder's hand. "We merely need your sustenance, or shall I find a wet-nurse instead?"

He halted, turned to the queen with confused eyes.

"Dawn, you will do as I command or your brother will inflict a horrid death upon that runt."

The prince came to his mother's side with a jeweled dagger oiled and ready. His face betrayed his pleasure.

"Mother! You would not dare!"

"Vane, prove why you are my favorite," the queen required. Her eyes flared behind her thin veil.

The prince brother bowed to a knee, kissed the cross about his mother's neck, then turned on his sister.

"Wait!" Dawn shrieked and stepped back into the elder who had blocked her retreat.

The prince's smile grew as he raised the knife.

"Wait!" she repeated with panic. "I will do it. I will take care of him myself." Tears of terror soaked her trembling cheeks.

Vane halted, offering his knife by the handle. "Do it then, Sister.

Kiss Mother's cross and show us you are her daughter."

"Not like this," Dawn wept. "I will give him to the wolves of the forbidden wood, where I found him."

Gnostro tilted his head with interest.

"You lie," the prince spouted. "Mother has said there are no wolves in those woods. Only disgraced men, like Cano, and their psilocybin dreams."

"But there are, Brother. If you would but venture beyond Mother's boundary, you would find this truth. Possibly others."

The prince huffed a hard breath, turned to his mother for a sign of what to do.

The queen remained still for a moment, then said to her daughter, "Very well, Lady Dawn. Slay this child of yours and I will favor you once more. Bring a token of the deed and my true favorite you will become."

Vane's face tightened like a castle preparing for assault. He shed a single tear, returned his dagger to his tri-point baldric strapped across his chest, and fled the court in visible displeasure.

On the back of her horse, with the contented baby in her arms, Dawn rode over the lowered bridge, through the winding village roads, and into the falling dusk, where she approached the edge of the misty woods. Instead of following the path into the heart of the forest, she veered to Cano's cabin, where thick charcoal smoke churned from his chimney and firelight illuminated the keyhole of his door.

The neighing of her horse summoned the rugged man dressed in gray wolf pelts held by cords of twine and leather. His feet and hands were covered, a wolfen-headed hood hung down his back, and his long brown hair was tangled from weeks of bath-free hard living. His peregrine darted from over his shoulder and took watch within a tree.

"My princess," he said with shock at her arrival then kneeled with bowed head. "How may I serve you?"

"I need you to protect this child as though he were my own."

"As you command, my lady," Cano replied with a voice like a renting oak tree. He extended his massive arms to accept the swaddled child. The babe cried when Dawn bent to release him and he turned to face his new keeper.

Cano nearly dropped the boy from fright. "This child is Mong!" His face went pale, his hands trembled.

"My dear, Cano. What has gotten hold of you? There are no Mong in the world. They are the stuff of myths and bedtime stories." The princess read his face for signs of eaten mushrooms.

"This is a Mong child, my princess," he said with sobering lucidity over growing infant cries. "Without a doubt. His eyes give it away, the unblinking blue-green. Look, they are ceaseless. We must kill it before it's too late."

"No!" she commanded to her surprise. "How can you be certain of this?" Her tone dwindled from embarrassment.

"Has this child slept since you've come to possess him?"

"No, not a single minute, now that you mention it."

"Mong," he said. "Where did you find it?"

"In a mound on the edge of the wood."

"In the old Mong lands?"

"I don't know."

"Are there more?"

"No, just him. I heard him crying in the forest and went to him."

"Amazing," he whispered with admiration as he studied the squealing baby, who gave him odd glares. "The ancient Mong realm is at the edge of the forest. The petrified remains of the violent ones are littered deep in the valley. But there has been no Mong life for many thousands of years. They are long extinct."

"Evidently not. We must keep him secret, my mother wishes him dead."

"Death for this one is a wise choice, my lady. He may look like a baby, but he is Mong. If we don't end his life now—while he's young—

then he will grow to destroy us all. The entire realm."

The princess studied the baby's face for a moment. His cheeks were pale and smooth, swollen and sweet. His two-tone eyes flicked between her and Cano as his tiny nose sniffled. He stopped crying when he saw her and began to smile.

"No," she said decisively with the same tone of command. "You will protect him with your life. When he grows, you will teach him your ways and those of the forest. I will return to see him soon when it is safe. But now I must leave with a token of his spilled blood. For my ruse I will sacrifice a single toe, nothing more." She wiped a tear from her watery eyes. "Though I cannot do it myself. Please, my dear Cano, sever it for me as my heart weeps too much for him already."

Without hesitation Cano nodded, withdrew a sharpened ashen metal blade affixed to an antler handle, and snipped off a pinky toe, causing a spurt of blood and a roaring cry from the babe. The boy's ceaseless eyes widened as bloody teeth shot out of his gums. His skin split apart revealing a muscular mass beneath that moved like fibrous coils. Cano dropped him into the grass with surprise, and the babe's body shook as his screams increased. After a moment the wounds fused shut leaving pink scars over a drastically enlarged body. The baby had nearly doubled in size and took the form of a small bald boy no younger than four. His toe had regrown and his blue-green eyes fell on Dawn again, calming him.

"My lady," the boy said with a subtle strain in his cherubim voice.

Cano's face had frozen with shock. His mouth hung open, and he did not move.

Dawn dismounted her horse to kneel before the handsome boy. She slowly picked up the baby's severed toe.

"My dear, you are wonderful," she said softly and took one of his hands in hers.

"This is not right, princess," Cano said at last. His voice wavered like a tree in a storm. "He will doom us."

"No, I think he's just perfect, and beautiful."

The boy hugged Dawn tight. His grip had strengthened to something like a man's. She hugged him in return, finding that his body had hardened with muscle despite his youthful image.

"Please," she said to him, "remain with my friend, Cano. He will teach you his ways, and I will visit you often. Can you do that for me?"

The boy relaxed his hug and stared deep into her eyes as she spoke. He nodded to her question, then turned to Cano, who shuddered under his unblinking gaze.

The princess kissed his forehead, tucked the baby toe into a crease of her plum corset, and remounted her horse. With a warm smile she vanished into the night on her way back to her mother's fortress.

TWO

On the morning of the first fortnight the princess left her writing to dry and found Cano's peregrine at her tower window. Its parchment payload requested her presence for unstated reasons, and she worried about the cause of such a brash act. As she sent the falcon away, a bolt pierced its breast and pinned it to her window frame in a plume of feathers. A cheer followed from the opposite tower's parapet, along with the distinct excessive boast of her prince brother.

"You really should be more careful, Sis," Vane shouted. "And what was that? Old Cano's playing for your hand again?" He raised his crossbow with a laugh and slapped the shoulder of the instructing guard captain next to him. "Doesn't he know you're mine?"

More laughter and agreeable cheer from the prince's men filled the morning air.

Dawn backed away from the window, weeping and horrified, and clutched the tiny note the woodsman had scrawled. She eyed the aged short sword her father had gifted before his wasting, traced the bead of jade that was affixed to the hilt, and eyed the rare ashen metal it was forged from. It matched the bead affixed to his own long sword that disappeared long ago. Her memory of his technique had faded; she had seen Cano practicing but was too afraid to try a stroke. She picked up the hem of her violet dress, brushed the black, lace veil from her eyes, and ran down the spiraling stone stairs with an anxious heart. Her pearls and beads rattled as she stepped. The knotted ashen metal cross her mother had given in exchange for the bloody token clanged on its chain. At the landing level she ran into the elder.

"Where are you off to, my dear princess? Have you already finished your daily scrivening?" Gnostro asked.

In the sunlight his gray beard was like the feral fur of a wolf in the forbidden wood. His crimson cape covered his slender shoulders, and his belly protruded under his green-and-gold uniform.

"How dare you ask my business, Servant," she said with increased confidence of command in the manner of her mother.

He bowed, red-faced with embarrassment, and moved out of her path.

Dawn smiled after passing and headed for the stable where she saddled her steed and rode out of the keep for the forbidden forest and Cano's cabin. By evening she arrived to a fire burning under roasted rabbits and two men swinging sparking swords together. Cano was clear in his wolfen clothing, but the other man, who she did not know, was a mountain of muscle with a dozen scars, huge and rugged, yet more handsome than any man in her realm. He wore a gray wolf fur around his loin but was otherwise naked with dark-brown hair that flowed to the middle of his back. He stood like the woodsman and moved like the wind, surprising him and Dawn both with a perfect replica of Cano's death fade. Using the signature defensive strike that arose from a feigned retreat, the massive man nicked the veteran up his chin with a live blade and sent him stumbling back, nearly falling into the flames.

"Cano!" Dawn called.

The two men stopped at the sound of her sharpened voice. Cano stood at attention with his blade between his feet and the hilt at his chest. A drop of blood fell from his chin; the mountain of a man training with him copied exactly and stood the same. As the man looked up, Dawn recognized his blue-green eyes and nearly fell from her horse.

"My princess, please," Cano said dropping his sword to rush to her aid.

The Mong man did the same without relinquishing his weapon and beat his teacher to her side. He lifted her with ease from the leather saddle. "My princess, please," he mirrored.

As he held her firm she peered into the black pupils of his unblinking eyes and could not fathom their depths. The strength of his arms and warmth of his body stripped her of the inward mask she had donned for the queen and allowed her to release a flood of ache and tears. She sobbed on his shoulder, held her face close to his flesh and while it had only been a fortnight, she felt she'd missed the young boy's entire life.

"Is it truly you?" she said so faintly only the Mong heard.

He nodded and held her still. Cano stared silently, then collected his sword and sat by the roasting rabbit. He sniffed the air and pulled a piece of meat from the carcass to feed himself. "Majesty, this is what I needed you to see."

The Mong lowered the princess to the ground, keeping eye contact. Dawn moved closer to the fire where she studied his body closely, touching every scar with her delicate fingers.

"How?" she asked Cano without looking at him.

"We've been working. Chopping wood for the fire, training with blades, and learning the way of the wild world. There were accidents, and each time his flesh was broken he grew rapidly into what you now see. This is still his infancy, my lady."

"Him? An infant?"

"Aye. And he knows more than he lets on. There is old knowledge in his blood."

"You are amazing," she whispered to the massive man with eyes of infatuation.

His gaze narrowed as from a severe pain, then relaxed again as he sighed heavily. The princess wondered at him.

"I am glad to have come, but we must continue to hide him," Dawn said to Cano. "Have you had visitors or wanderers in the woods?"

"Two days ago, a triad of the prince's bowmen came looking for fawn and left with a pair. Probably for His Majesty's perverse pleasures. I hid the Mong behind the falls nearby."

The massive man broke his gaze from Dawn when Cano said *Mong*.

"Mong," he repeated. "What is Mong?"

Cano's eyes tensed. He was fearful to share the stories. To ease his worry, he withdrew a reedless flute and blew a fast but sorrowful melody that rode the night winds and stirred the princess's heart.

"They are your people," Dawn said with a warm smile and took the massive man's hand in hers while she moved to Cano's tune by the firelight.

"Where are my people?"

"You are the very last," she said with a frown while spinning. She closed her eyes, let the music wash over her, and stepped closer to the massive man.

He nodded and stabbed his sword into the soft soil where it stood strong. "The very last," he repeated to himself while staring at her beautiful dance.

There was something about his demeanor and appearance that softened Dawn's heart. She stopped her motion to sit close to him and pressed her shoulder against his, feeling his warmth through her royal dress.

"I am sad to be the last," he said with unblinking eyes.

Cano cut off his tune, raised an eyebrow with intrigue.

"We are here with you," she said. "While you are the last of your people, you will not walk alone in the world. I am with you always."

The words pierced Cano through his heart, where a secret desire had grown and now died. The woodsman rose from the fire with a mouthful of rabbit, bowed to the princess, and offered her privacy by retreating to his cabin. There, under the milky light of the moon, the princess laid down with the last Mong in the soft grasses of Cano's camp and followed the fluttering fireflies flying over them. She held his hardened hand and touched his chiseled cheek with her soft palm, turned his noble face toward her, and stared into his fathomless, unclosing eyes. She dared to kiss him and they embraced, sharing the evening in a moment of miraculous love.

THREE

VANE SENT A SILENT signal with a jeweled hand. His captain passed the order to his crossbowmen and they moved into position around his sleeping sister and her lover. He spied the glowing cabin with ash plumes rising from the chimney and the smoldering fire pit outside. A charred carcass hung motionless over it.

"Fire!" Vane shouted with a sinister smile.

A torrent of loosed bolts peppered the woodsman's home, the trees behind it, and the dying fire site. A giant of a man hopped up from the grass with alarm as he was struck several times with blistering iron. He swiped at his body as though it were burning and roared an admirable roar that shook the prince's resolve, made him question his safety for a moment. "Nock!" he called to his men with a crack in his commanding voice.

Dawn cried out in response to the hulk's roar. Her silhouette, recognizable by the flowing royal gown, scrambled to the cabin in a crouch.

"Again! Fire!" Vane yelled with traces of fear. After a slight delay, a stream of bolts blanketed the cabin and its surroundings a second time. The enormous man leaped in front of the princess to shield her, caught a dozen more bolts in his chest and half as many in his abdomen. He fell to the ground and rolled to his back, bellowing in pain.

The prince's pride returned. "Sister! That was a close one!" Vane laughed over the moans of the fallen man who appeared as a mound in the grass. "Mother is going to hear about this! Lying with a pagan in the wood, and not even that hound Cano. Your reputation may fall further than I expected."

In a moment the clinks and plinks of cocked crossbows accompanied the prince's laughter. "Shoot that poor fool," he said to his captain and savored the whisking boltwind that blew by. With thunks the missiles struck the whole field where the nude warrior fell, saturating his body until the pelt-covered woodsman burst from the tree-plank door howling like a wolf and firing a bow made from an oak branch. His sole arrow slew one of Vane's men, and he flung the weapon aside to draw two short daggers from his waist. He charged the arbalists in vain, took thrice bolts to his face, and fell under continued barrage until he was like a pulpy cushion full of pins. His furs soaked with blood, his face stuck down in the grass.

The royal sister screamed at the woodsman's death. Her shrill voice cut the air like a guillotine, and being vulnerable and alone, she fled for the tree line.

"There's no sense in running, my lovely sister!" Vane snickered. To his captain he ordered: "Bring me their heads. I wish to sip my evening soup from their skulls."

The captain passed word, and a dozen men put down their crossbows to draw short swords and move in for the butchery. They stepped sideways over Cano's corpse, sawed his head from his shoulders, and tossed it back toward Vane. They moved next for the beast of a man writhing by the dying fire and full of projectiles. Surprised by his resilience, they held their blades at the ready.

Without warning the naked man pushed up to his side and tore a handful of bolts from his mangled chest with a roar. The men stopped in horror as he rose to tower over them, now doubled in size. With a giant fist he grabbed the nearest man and hurled him at his comrades, stomped another into a flat mess, and pitched the broken bolts at the remaining men, who turned to flee, screaming for their prince and captain.

Vane, feeling dizzy, panicked and fell over backwards frightened. The sounds of the fight blurred with his vision, and a pungent smell stung his nose. His hands had become sticky with a viscous slime, and he screamed like a little boy.

His captain ignored the weakness and drew his own sword in futile bravery while they watched the crazed shouting giant brutalize everyone in his path on a charge to their position. Hurled limbs and chunks of guards heralded the onslaught, followed by a war cry that soiled the prince's trousers and sent him running for his royal life. Crumpling armor, loosed crossbows, and shouts cut short drove him to run faster until the carnage and his captain were gone. All he heard was his own pounding heart.

Alone in the dark wood, Vane froze. The shadows blended with the moonlight to create a squirming scene full of liquefied trees, melting flora, and glistening eyes that opened and closed all around him. He struggled to catch his breath, rubbed his forehead, and smeared the slime across his mouth. He spit out the bitter substance and tried to calm himself. He reflected on what had happened, his heart quickened with confusion.

"Mother!" he shouted senselessly and floundered zig zag through the worn path like a lunatic.

FOUR

THE PRINCESS WEPT BESIDE a trickling brook, her tears merged with the flowing waters of the deep forest. The image of Cano's death and the abominable Mong broke her heart, twisted her stomach, and interrupted her mourning with bouts of nausea. She wiped her swollen pink eyes with mud-caked hands and fell to her back on the rocky bed of the stream. She listened to the gurgling churn and stared up through the canopy at the blue-and-white sky, longing for a conversation with her betrayed father. Her torn gown was half submerged and tugged on her with the ebb of the current.

She stirred from a slight vibration in the tranquil air that was at first too subtle to knowingly detect but quickly grew in strength and frequency. She heard it then like the beating of a heavy drum. A chorus of snapping trees joined in, and within moments there was a visible disturbance at the edge of her sight. Something massive broke through the forest like an unstoppable wave of devastation, crushing and destroying everything in its path.

Dawn rose to her feet, afraid and defeated, refusing to run from her death. She pulled her sopping dress behind her and stood boldly, resolved to die by the terrible force moving toward her. She saw feet and knees and something towering above the treetops and realized it was the Mong. He had grown orders larger since the early evening ambush. A weight fell from her shoulders, excitement bubbled in her heart, but she was still cautious and unsure if he was the man she loved or a savage warmonger warned about in legend.

"My love!" she cried with a tender, weeping voice and eyes soaked with pain.

The pounding footfalls halted, and the enormous form of a man fell to a knee, shaking the quiet brook. "My princess," said a deafening voice from above the leaves. An enormous head lowered and searched with unblinking blue-green eyes.

Upon seeing the familiar stare, her love welled inside and she burst with tears of joy, ran to his bent face, and tried to hug it with futility. Her arms partially stretched across a single cheek, and he gently nudged her in return. He sucked in the air around her, blowing her hair about, and strained to whisper.

"My princess, it is you," he said in the softest voice he could find. "Cano is lost. I feared you were too."

"My brother and his men found us. Vane the Spiteful, whose jealousy and stupidity know no bounds."

"Vane," the Mong repeated.

"Raised by my mother and her death cultists. He will come searching for me. What shall we do?"

The titanic face of the Mong remained calm. He sucked in more air and whispered over his princess: "Fear not, my love. For you have the last Mong fighting on your side. Give me your command and I will annihilate your mother, brother, and all of their death cultists in an instant." His voice rose with anger, blowing the princess off balance and sending her tumbling backward. He stood to full height, disappeared above the trees, and shouted a great shout that rang louder than anything Dawn had ever witnessed. The ground broke open from its force, the trees bent in half, and her body felt a shock as though she'd been dropped from a great height.

"Please," she mumbled, trying to stay conscious. "I can't—"

The Mong's rage had dissolved his control over his voice, and pure hatred erupted from his mouth like spewed magma. When it stopped, everything was dead silent, and he scrambled to find his lovely princess among the wreckage.

"My lady, I am sorry!" he whispered frantically and lowered his head. His hands sifted the broken timbers until he found her limp and unmoving. He lifted her high off the ground and carried her deeper into the forest with a heavy heart seared with fire. "Your ears and body are frail compared to mine, and I must learn to guard against myself so as to not extinguish your beautiful light." He spoke aloud despite her incapacitation.

After summiting the tall mounds that surrounded the base of a giant mountain, the Mong rested unknowingly in the long-forgotten kingdom of his petrified ancestors. He lowered his princess into a soft, shaded space next to a small waterfall, allowing her to recover.

"If your queen mother is our enemy, my love, who will hunt for you no matter where you go, then we have but a single choice: I will make my people's art against her in your name, and you will rule as my empress when I have completed my work."

This he promised her.

FIVE

"But, mother," Vane whined. His tears cut lines in the smeared yellowish mud caked across his face. "It was not my fault. There was a giant in the woods! He killed them all, even that old fool, Cano! If I hadn't been brave enough to—"

"Silence," the queen commanded from her seat of power. She kept her placid composure despite a broken sleep of night terrors, and she sat like a stoic statue speaking with a voice of glacial ice. Her purple gown was decorated with tiny finger bones strung together to make an elaborate necklace that rattled with death on the slightest movement. Her twisted cross and enveloped black orb hung between her breasts, two tiny skulls decorated her shoulders as morbid pauldrons, and an ashen metal crown rested on her tied-back hair. Her face was painted snow white, except for black accents around her eyes, and her lips were painted blood red with cinnabar rouge.

"Gnostro," she called.

He appeared from the rear court entrance and hurried to her aide.

"Majestic Highness, how may I—your mortal instrument—serve your divine will?" Neither his eyes nor voice gave indication that he heard her early morning screams. He addressed her with dignity.

"When am I to receive the dread lord Mawveth? You summoned him yesterday when we heard the thunder coming from the ancient Mong kingdom."

"My queen, he entered our boundaries yesterday evening with his convoy, and will be upon us before dusk. A pair of heralds and their escort have already arrived."

"Bring them to me." Her icy words raised the hairs on Gnostro's neck.

"Of course, my lady," he said with an awkward swallow and departed.

"Mother, please—"

The queen silenced her strained son with a sharp stare.

In moments the elder returned, followed by two black shades who crept under hooded robes dark as the void. They were silent save their labored breaths and the bones they concealed that rattled out of sight. The hem of their garments swept the floor behind them as the court doors sealed shut.

On seeing their entry the queen stiffened her spine, erected her neck in a display of power. "You two wraiths, where is Lord Mawveth? When will he arrive?"

They remained silent.

The queen shot a glare at Gnostro, who cleared his throat with anxiety and addressed the shadowed duo.

"My dearest friends, please understand our queen is quite eager to know the whereabouts of her daughter, to hear your thoughts on the disturbing tales of our prince, and to know what you make of the thunder that came from the forest today with clear skies. We are in need of your wisdom. Please dispel our confusion." Gnostro bowed low as he finished his oration.

The wraith next to him turned without lifting its hood. "Disturbing tales indeed," he said with a voice like grinding glass.

"Tell them of the story relayed by my son, of this giant in the wood," the queen said.

"My lady, the telling is hard to decipher and we must exercise caution. The spores of that forest, which are on your son's face, have made him see all manners of things. Men go mad in that place, hallucinating all kinds of terrors. We can't know for certain until I test his blood."

"Call me a liar again, old man, and I'll sleep in your skin after sundown," scathed the prince as he reclined against the base of the black throne. "And I'll drink your blood as my wine." He leaned into his mother's dress like an infant needing comfort. She placed a cold hand on his matted caramel hair.

"Our knights have already ascertained this knowledge," said the second wraith from under her hood. Her voice was like a shrieking cat that echoed eerily in the court chamber.

Gnostro shifted uncomfortably and tugged at the collar of his cape to cool himself. Dark spots of sweat saturated his uniform. "And what was discovered?" he asked with a timid softness.

"That a Mong lives, and it was the venting of a great rage that you took for thunder earlier this morning."

Stray courtiers wandered closer, and the prince jerked upright with full attention. Whispers filled the room.

"A Mong?" the queen asked.

The wraiths turned toward her but kept silent.

"That's absurd," Gnostro said. "There are no more Mong. Haven't been for fifty generations. Your knights must have been inebriated."

At the sound of the elder's doubt, the court doors flung open and in flowed a stinking gust of death followed by a half dozen heavily armored black knights stomping into the center. Their oxide plates were blacker than the wraiths' robes and resounded with each step.

Fully-grown skulls were affixed to their shoulders and smaller, younger skulls, which matched the queen's pauldrons, hung from chains on their belts. Images of younglings being tortured and sacrificed were proudly embossed on their chests. The golden hilts of their long swords were decorated with dark runes. They assembled in a triangle formation behind the wraith magi, their leader stood proud with a skull standard affixed to a wooden pole on his back.

"Our knights," the first wraith said with crackling words and a frail white hand gesturing to the warriors, "have immunity to the psilocybin flourishing in the ancient wild lands. With lucid eyes we have found the wreckage and tracks of an adolescent Mong near a lone cabin where the wolves do not venture. The remains of many men openly rot in the sun there."

"It would have been a glorious battle," moaned the head knight through his iron face shield. He blew a disgusting sigh of anguish through the twisted cross that was cut from the front. Wild ruby eyes, a sharp nose, and burgundy lips that moved over plum-stained teeth were faintly visible underneath. The knights around him shuddered with muted excitement. Some gripped the hilts of their weapons to satisfy the bloodlust boiling within.

The queen remained still. "Where is your lord and commander?"

"Mawveth will meet you when the sun has fallen to the abyss. The void night inspires us, and Mawveth moves under its protection," said the first wraith.

"He has much to deal with you, Queen of Nightmares," said the second. "Be ready for him."

To the prince's shock, the queen nodded. A wide-eyed sense of awe grew over him as the six death knights saluted the wraiths, then parted to let them pass between their ranks on the way out of the court chamber. The knights followed, along with their pervasive aura of death and fear.

Vane's mood lifted as soon as they vanished.

Later that night, when the castle torches were lit and the stars were bright in the sky, trumpets sounded from the grand entrance professing a highborn arrival. With patience she sat until at last the tall, crowish lord threw open her chamber door and strode into the center with his armored hands behind his plated back. A gleaming knotted cross was bolted to his breast yet empty of a black orb, and a long dagger was sheathed on his right ribs. Two dark metal swords hung from his waist—the longer one had a jade stone affixed to its hilt. Skulls and deathly imagery adorned his armor, and his black-bearded face lurched forward like a corvus seeking carrion. His long, black hair grew in clumps like hanging feathers. A host of wraiths and knights followed him.

"Narcene, you owe me for what I am about to do," he said with a slow, edgy voice that left his audience feeling uneasy. He rested a hand on the jeweled sword's pommel.

The queen made no reply. She gazed with empty eyes.

"I, Mawveth, the Lord of Dread, come here equipped to save this realm and the entire world from a threat you cannot hope to overcome. It is I, and my legion, who have the old knowledge, the old defenses against this impossible titan you now face. We are all that can save you."

The queen's court was paralyzed. Silence filled the periphery.

"But before I share how I'm going to deal with this youngling Mong of yours, you must guarantee my reward."

"Name your price," the queen said.

"When he's felled, I will take the virgin Dawn and the rest of your house for myself with the blessing of the fiefdoms. The Mong's body will belong to me."

"What for?" asked Gnostro with a painful apprehension in his face.

"We will mine his bones and brain for the potent rarities they are, his skin will be made into parchment and sacks for our sacrifices to stay warm during my rituals. The wee ones shiver as they go under the knife, as you may recall during your coronation."

The queen glanced at the bone on her shoulder, shuddered with a passing thought, but kept quiet and nodded.

"How might you plan to do such a deed?" asked Gnostro weakly from the perimeter of the court behind the dark lord. "What are all the contraptions you have wheeled here? Vats of poison? And you've brought the large darkstone. Tell us your intent—do you wish to inflict nightmares upon us all?"

Mawveth glared at the elder and froze him with fear. By the time Gnostro had thawed, the dread lord had long departed without explanation.

SIX

"WHAT NAME DO YOU like, my love?" sang the princess from the highest branch in the highest tree of the mound lands that sprawled beyond the mountain's base. She smiled into the unblinking eyes of the Mong and basked in the warm sun. "There is Elkh or Khairon or Melekhor. The names of my father's line, which you should take if we are to wed."

With a soft smile and controlled whisper, the Mong replied, "I feel my people had their own names, but I do not know them. So, tell me of your father and his fathers before him."

The princess was delighted to recount the tale of her beloved sire until a black arrow pierced the canopy and struck the Mong in the side of his neck. He started with surprise and bit down on his rage to protect the princess. He turned to look from where it had come and swept a massive hand through the trees, knocking them down and revealing the heavy, labored grunts of dying men.

The princess screamed with alarm and slid down the trunk of the great tree as another black arrow sailed true, landing on the other side of the Mong's larynx. The Mong scrambled and smashed the forest around him, careful to avoid the tree where he had hid the princess.

His heels drove many stoutly armored shadows into the soil, crushing them flat. Facing away from the tall tree, the Mong vented his rage to the ground and shook the forest for miles before he made large sweeping motions with his limbs and cleared whole acres with each swipe.

Another arrow hissed from behind, pierced the nape of his neck, and forced a blinding fury that he could not control. His blue-green eyes glazed, and the true nature of the Mong erupted. Like a fanatic of war killing all in its path, he tore up the great tree and swung it just as Cano had taught him. He then made great strokes against the ground to kill his enemies, who scrambled like tiny black ants that poured over his feet and flung ashen spears into his flesh.

Amid the blurry battle, the Mong's neck became hot and burned with chemical fire. He swiped at it but could not stop the spread. It streamed into his head and face, down his arms and chest, and shot through his legs seizing him with rigorous agony. His jaw clenched and he could not yell, but tipped backward and fell into the mountain, rolled down and settled at its base. The tiny black ants clamored all over him with piercing spears and ashen swords that hacked away his skin, and spread the poison further.

The princess let out a devastating cry near his paralyzed face until an obsidian gauntlet muffled her voice and she was carried off by a shadow of a knight.

As the ropes were heaped about the Mong's throat and logs rushed beneath him, he felt the hateful poison diffusing deeper into his body until he lost all control and was enveloped by an endless sea of pain.

SEVEN

THE PRINCESS TORE OFF the skirt and sleeves of her royal gown and wrapped it around the poker of her bed chamber's hearth. She stabbed it into the fire, lit the material, and threw it on her bed. Red-faced and streaming tears, she dragged her wardrobe cabinet from the wall and tipped it into the kindled flame, then pulled the heirloom tapestries from their mountings to hurl them atop as well.

To death I will follow him, she told herself with bitterness. "Father, keep me in your guard," she prayed aloud. "Ease the suffering that is coming to me, if that is my fate. I will meet it bravely as you have already done."

Clothes, bedding, the remaining wooden furniture were all heaped upon the growing blaze. Fearless and angry, she took up the sword her father had given her as a young girl, drew it from the scabbard, and inspected it for readiness just as he'd shown her. Without oil it had rusted along its guard and ridge, but the fullers on both sides were clear of corrosion, and its edge had held sharp against the long neglect.

She tested its weight with two diagonal cuts, just as she'd been taught long ago, and jabbed open her window with its point. The black clouds billowed into the sky over the amassing armies who had marched from all the neighboring fiefdoms to see the last Mong. A few heads turned at her ruckus before she ducked out of sight. She hid near her locked iron door awaiting the first guard to enter.

In a minute the room had become hot with fire that spread onto the stone floor. Her face burned, and her torn clothes singed as the flame spread and snapped at her feet. She withheld the urge to scream, scolded herself for her carelessness, and sucked up the feeble fright that no longer made sense to her. The princess died in that moment, a victim of the damned queen and her death knight poison. Now she was something else that had no title: a bare woman intent on revenge.

The outside bolts of her lock slid open with a loud screeching echo. The heavy door was pushed open, and inside stepped a trio of guards softly calling for the princess Dawn. With a hard heart she slid her sword into the side of the first, then faded back as the second leaped for her. With a vicious scream and blinding upward cut, she caught the guard under his chin to the bridge of his nose. He fell face-first at her feet gushing and struggling. She stepped barefoot off his back and lunged for the third guard who blocked her aged blade with his unarmored forearms. The edge cut clean through taking off his hands. He yelled at the sudden turn of luck, then shouted for help as the first guard, who gripped his leaking ribs, fell into the fire.

More lightly armored footsteps came from the hall with a confirming yell. Another guard entered the room, horrified by the flaming soldier and the second guard bleeding from his face.

"Get her, you prat!" the third guard, handless and desperate, cried to bring the fourth to his senses.

The fourth guard shook off the stun and drew his short sword.

It was regular steel, forged in the normal way, and would not stand up to her ashen edge. He dashed forward with a stabbing thrust. But the princess feigned in Cano's way, and rose her blade high through the new man's elbows, sending his gripped sword flying into the immolating first guard, knocking them both out the open window. While the fourth guard stared horrified at his maimed arms, she made a second diagonal cut down his left shoulder and buried her edge in his torso past his spine. She braced his body with her foot and pushed to free her blade from him.

The third guard, sweating with stress and shock, circled away from her holding his bleeding wrist-stumps close. He hurried toward the door to flee.

She dashed in front of him, sword point inches from his eyes.

He raised his bleeding, handless arms and halted, tilted his head, and wept for sympathy.

She pressed the point to the man's throat, leaning him painfully backward while she pulled his blade from its scabbard and held it ready in a two-sword guard that she had watched Cano use once in solo practice.

She backed out of the room and slammed the door shut, but did not bother to lock it. She fled down the spiral stairs of her tower stopping to find a squad of yelling guards clamoring up to her level. She decided to climb to the roof instead. Once through the doors at the top she stabbed her stolen weapon through the handles to lock it shut.

Desperate and prepared to die, she stood atop the parapets nearly breathless and gazed down at the spectacle below. Her old sword stuck to her hand, she squeezed it with vengeance.

Never had she seen the Mong from such a height; his size had become truly terrifying and spanned several neighboring fiefs. Outside the castle walls his body had been entrenched with diggers expanding the resting place and clearing trees as he grew from trauma. She could see his active blue-green eyes darting around with lucidity as his body was sedated and tied down with great cables made of many ropes braided together. A small village had been built atop his chest, and great holes were made all through him to allow for the mining of his diamond-marrowed bones using Mawveth's ashen tools. His wounds dripped with vast volumes of blood that were caught in wheeled vessels hauled by slaves overseen by the death knights. The sanguine fluid was carted to a congregation of black-cloaked wraiths who surrounded a large darkstone and who poured the precious flow over the orb, causing it to glow a glimmering white beneath the spattering. The blood and light soon vanished with splintering offshoots of ashen mineral forming in their place. They then performed the ritual again chanting a low, hateful song, which entranced them as more metal emerged from the dark sphere.

Congregant wraiths also coated the mouths of the mining holes with a beryl balm that smoked on contact with the Mong's broken flesh. More death knights had gathered around the Mong's head and forced conscripted townsfolk to pump green fluids into his arteries with soft vessels sewn of fawnskin. Dawn's heart broke at the sight of her tormented and exploited love, and she nearly flung herself from the tower in despair. She stayed her suicide with the image of her mother's triumphant grin and turned to the towering spire that rose behind her. She knew her mother was in the apex chamber watching the evil endeavors of her knights. She made peace with never seeing her mother or brother again and returned her empty stare to the sensational suffering on the ground.

The Mong's massive eyes twitched and flicked about with agony, until they spied her and remained locked. She felt something stir her heart like a secret wind gusting through her, and her pulse quickened with the realization that his sensitive eyes were watching her from so far away. Great glass tears shed from his ducts causing an unexpected frenzy among the wraiths to catch the ultra-rarities. They scolded the knights, who scrambled to preserve every precious ounce in tankards, bowls, and half-empty mugs. They drank the tears and made cheers to each other before continuing their forced infections of his blood.

"My love," she wept.

"Go to him," whispered the flat voice of a man from behind that startled the princess, causing her to slip from the rooftop. She fell with a piercing scream and twisted to glimpse a flat, black silhouette of a man—much like the one she'd encountered in the forbidden wood—who had been standing silent behind her and then vanished into smoke.

Her scream cut the still air and turned every head on the ground, including those of the knights and wraiths who toiled over the suspended body of the last Mong.

The blue-green eyes caught every moment of her doom, and the Mong's heart responded to her scream. It triggered an unprecedented violence within him that boiled his blood and vaporized the coursing toxins. In an instant his body exploded inside forcing great geysers of material and miners to blow out of his wounds. He jerked upright with such fervor that he broke his restraints and sent the thousands of oppressors camping on his chest flying to their deaths. He reached out his massive left hand and caught the falling princess, safely sealing her in his enormous fist like a tiny seed of narrow-leafed campion.

"My princess," he boomed.

With a new kind of fire burning in his chest and a restored strength from the purging of the poison, the last Mong rolled over and labored to push up to his swelling feet despite the roaring tumult among the men clamoring around him. Futile spears, arrows, and slung stones bounced harmless off his regenerating skin. Each wound only made him grow larger, and with two stomps he annihilated the main forces assailing him and snuffed out all the knights who remained. The survivors fled, scattering like insects.

With princess in hand, the Mong stood erect and looked down

on the castle's spire. His rage bubbled inside. He crouched to see into the tallest chamber and found the wicked queen naked and in the act of a depraved ritual with Mawveth. The two had consummated their sanctioned union and were unprepared for the rising of their captives. Mawveth had no armor and entered the balcony naked, except for his pride.

The Mong raised his hand to sweep them from the world, but the shriek of his love stayed his smite.

"No!" the princess cried from inside the shelter of his other hand. He opened it briefly to look at her, and she jabbed a finger toward the spire while calling for her mother.

He held her out to see them in their act of desecration. "Why, Mother?" Dawn called with a voice like a bolt of lighting. "Why have you done this to us?"

The naked queen stepped into the open, her long black hair hung over her aged curves. She wore no makeup, nor royal accents or trinkets. She too was bare and human.

All around the castle below, the armies of the surrounding kingdoms gathered. Their war machines were rolled into place, catapults were loaded, fearful knights on horseback waited with drawn futile weapons.

"Bring me to her," the princess said while squeezing her sword's hilt.

The Mong lowered his head to Dawn from the wispy clouds, forced a quietness in his voice that still staggered her strong stance with whipping winds, "Must you risk yourself, my lady? Why should I not end this now?"

"Because I must be the one to face her, not you," she said while standing firm. "And her demon lover, the betrayer of my father."

"Then for my part I will destroy all those who have helped her and those who have helped them."

"No," commanded the princess. She touched his hardened face and stared with calm eyes that sparkled like diamonds. "For they will become mine after *I* have completed *my* work." She smiled a sorrowful smile and turned to face her mother. The Mong obeyed and carefully moved her closer to the spire where the queen retreated a step, while Mawveth held his ground.

"Come, Mother, if you wish to control me—to dictate what I am to be—then try it now!" Dawn called from the Mong's steady palm. Her ripped gown fluttered in the high winds contouring her petite, muscular frame. Her torn sleeves revealed strong, beautiful arms that had swelled from the few minutes spent wielding her sword. She was proud and bold without the weighted clutter of her mother's garb. The twisted metal cross about her neck swayed, she tore it free breaking its clasp, and cast it off the Mong's hand down to the ground. Sword first, she stepped onto the stone platform of the spire top. Her face stiffened.

Wide-eyed with fury, the queen stole an ashen metal dagger from among Mawveth's clothes and faced her daughter with it concealed behind her back. She stood erect in the way of her rule despite being naked.

"What do you think you're doing, Daughter?" she said with a cold, unwavering glare.

"I should ask you the same thing!" Dawn said crying and held her short sword in front of her.

The queen looked upon its tip, then matched Dawn's stare. Through their eyes they pushed on each other with competing pressure, trying to break the other's will. "After your whole life, all I've done for you—carried you, birthed you, nursed and raised you—you would put this weapon to me?"

The princess cried but held her gaze and guard. She restrained her words, thought only of her father's burial and the sour-smelling spore that floated out of the forest that day and across a wide meadow that lead to the majestic burial hills where he was laid. After the ritual her mother had warned her never to enter the woods, for there were wolves and worse lurking about.

"You look just like him, you know," the queen said with disgust. She raised the ashen dagger like a large metal fang. "He gave me that same face when he found my hand behind his poisoning. He cried, and wept. But begged for *your* life."

Dawn blinked. She shook with a deep sadness, and her face flushed.

"And now you, my child, turn on your mother! For a man—if that's what you call it." She shot her tear-glazed eyes up toward the enormous being towering over her. "You can never be with him!" she said with disgust. "He is an abomination. Doomed to live and die alone in this world."

"No, Mother. He is not alone, and I am already one with him." The princess touched her stomach while keeping her sword steady.

The queen stepped closer and stared, then clenched her jaw. She held her composure for a moment then charged screaming with her blade slashing through the air.

Dawn used Cano's footwork to step out of her way but spared her the death blow. Yet she did not stop her fall over the edge of the sky-scraping spire, spewing spiteful curses and turning the sacrificial blade on herself before hitting the ground.

Mawveth's eyes widened and shot between the princess and the fathomless Mong towering among clouds above them. He fell to a knee, lowered his head.

"My queen," he said to Dawn, then hesitated. "I am yours to command."

Dawn sobbed. To her surprise, Mawveth's words were more powerful than her mother's fall. In the span of two moments her mind filled with faint memories from her earliest years—her father's smile, him holding her high in the sunlight, his long ashen sword swinging through the air, the moment he gave her the blade she now carried. They were followed by visions of her young mother, a cheerful maiden wrapped in purple and smiling. But then thoughts of Mawveth invaded, who similarly invaded their fief and house, throwing them into darkness with their blood-metal weapons and freakish fanatic warriors. A streak of sorrow ran through her heart, and she wanted to fall to her knees crying out her father's name. But with a strengthened will she controlled herself, turning her focus back to the evil standing before her.

"Then I command you to follow my mother." She said flatly and lowered her sword.

Mawveth lifted his head with a pained look of despair and paralysis. He hesitated.

She waited, and then said, "You, the lord of dread who takes so freely the lives of children and innocents, now hesitate to take your own life?" Her voice rose.

A boyish laugh bubbled from the dark shadows of the chamber. Vane stumbled onto the balcony with a dash of yellow across his lips and a handful of half-eaten psilocybin in his fist.

"Sister," he giggled. "What is the meaning of your intrusion? We had a glorious evening planned, and I was promised a bath in the Mong's blood. Mother was even going to let me use her darkstone. But here you are ruining everything." He hiccuped and steadied himself.

"You fool," she scolded with swollen eyes. "Mawveth—"

The tone in her voice raised the death knight commander's head with attention.

"Slay this foolish boy," she said with a harder heart. "Then follow my mother as I've ordered. Do not make me say it again."

Mawveth rose to his feet and stalked to Vane, who smiled at him gleefully while hands wrapped around his neck. With a yank and a snap, the knight killed the prince and tossed his body from the spire. Again despair flooded his face, and his eyes turned gray. He clenched his jaw and obeyed his new queen abandoning his life and stepping off the balcony without a word.

The princess sighed in her solitude on the breezy platform. Her salty tears chilled her cheeks in the wind. The Mong stood over her like a patient mountain, waiting for instructions.

Dawn walked to her father's sword resting against the wall of the royal gazebo. It was shades of dark gray along the grain and shimmered with oil. Its hilt matched her own smaller weapon's. On the face of the crossguard was a stone of polished jade, green and gleaming. She took the relic by the sling around its upper blade and cinched it to her back. She felt a great relief, despite its heavy weight.

Searching her mother's day bed under Mawveth's tunic, Dawn found her mother's twisted metal cross, which held a small darkstone. The necklace was coiled atop a cryptic scarlet codex. On its front cover was embedded another small darkstone the size of a marble. She took the book, seized her mother's chain, and squeezed its icy, black treasure in her palm. The metal bit her flesh, letting blood on the sphere and causing it to shine for a second. The tips of her fingers felt the orb's coldness, and she resolved to face the rumored nightmares that accompany its possession. Putting the chain around her neck, she returned to the towering Mong with closure.

He lowered his humongous hand, and she stepped into it. He elevated her to his shoulder where she saw the tiny specks of men below organizing for war. The perspective was exhilarating, and she felt a closeness to the Mong being at his height.

"I must speak to them," she said. "Please, call for silence."

The Mong nodded, creating a gust of wind that flapped her frayed royal dress and tested her balance. He gently raised her high into the air above his head. With earth-quaking steps that scattered the feeble warriors below, he turned and stood before the mighty castle of the vanquished queen and called down with a voice like thunder that blew through the men, shaking trees and homes in all the villages of the realm.

"Behold your new ruler," he blasted, "the Empress Dawn, who

with a single word can bless me to end your entire world." He heaved another lungful of air and displayed his empress over them with great pride.

Fresh tears streamed down her face from the Mong's heraldry. She stood in silence for a minute feeling the winds whip at her, pushing against her father's swords and against the dress tattered from war. After a deep breath she was ready. She signaled the Mong, who lowered her. With a clear voice she called down to the specks of people.

"Hear me, lords and ladies of my assembled fiefdoms. From this day forward you will pay tribute to me and you will kneel before my husband, the last of his people."

The assembly below restrained their weapons, looked among each other with dread, and one by one bent their knees to Dawn with lowered heads. Gnostro stood watching from afar on the smokey parapet of Dawn's lesser tower.

"My lady!" he called.

She turned at his voice, corrected him: "I am your empress now, Elder."

The Mong turned his stare on the old servant, who shuddered with terror from its weight.

"I will take up my throne elsewhere, in the land of the great mounds beyond the forbidden forest, which the legends say is the kingdom of the Mong. There I will form the seat of my empire and right the wrongs my mother made against my father's house." With a deep breath and heavy sigh, the princess turned to her love. "Tear this tainted monument of death to the ground."

The Mong obeyed, and with a single stroke of his free hand he knocked down the stone towers and great spire that had been built by her forefathers to stand for millennia. It crumbled in a rising mushroom cloud of stone, dust, and mortar. The myriad peoples of the realm shrieked and scrambled for their lives.

The empress led the last Mong away from the ruins, through the lush forest, and toward the tall mountains where his ancestors were said to have lived and died. They entered a valley full of hundreds of mounds of varying sizes covered with grass and trees. Near a river on the far side of the dell was the largest mound of all. The Mong strode to it, and the empress was pleased with the choice. He lowered her onto its crest, and with a heavy smile she walked holding her womb. She prayed to the whisper that had initiated her destiny in the forest and the sable statue that accompanied it.

"My love," she said after her prayer.

The Mong bent low to hear the soft voice of his empress.

"This is where our family will grow and where we will write the songs of our souls intertwined."

"Then here is where I will build you a fortress worthy of your empire," the Mong whispered without breath. He rose from his crouch and said at full strength, "And ours will be songs of triumph." He thundered over to the nearest mound and with two devastating holds, tore the barrow open from the top, peeling each side backward. Within was a large darkstone sphere, matte and shineless, encased in metal that ran deep underground. He tore the orb and metal from their place, bleeding from the jagged grasp, and set it at the base of their chosen plot, which he left undisturbed. He went to the next mound and did the same, adding it to the pile. When all the nearby mounds were clear, he returned to his empress and found her swinging her newfound blade. An alpha wolf, backed by its pack, lunged for her, and with a downward stroke, Dawn splayed its head from crown to chin. The surrounding wolves lowered their ears and snouts and whined for their fallen leader as Dawn readied her short sword in a natural guard, waiting to strike. The pack turned and ran down the tall slope, tails between their legs.

With a passing smile the Mong quaked over to the largest mountain and, starting at the top, began quarrying enormous stones.

Acknowledgements

I would like to thank you, the reader, for checking out this story. I hope you enjoyed it. If you did, **please take a quick moment to leave a review** where you purchased it!

I'd also like to thank my wife again, for being a constant source of strength. And my kids, who have taught me the meaning of perseverance.

A special thanks to Jonathan Starke. I really appreciated your help, surgical eye, and tales of Europe that I enjoyed from the dark corners of my writing space.

And thanks to Scott Alexander Jones and Darko Tomic for your help in making this book.

Email List Sign-Up

If you'd like to read more of my stuff (some even weirder than this!) or keep track of more of my content activity, check out my personal website at https://caseybrandt.com. From there you can sign up for my mailing list to keep up to date on new work, participate in feedback collection, access preview content, and more!

About the Author

Casey Brandt is a writer and senior software professional. He lives in the Austin, Texas area with his wife and four kids. He received his undergraduate degree in English Writing from the University of Nevada, Reno and is a lifelong learner. When not reading, writing, or making things, he is usually laughing with his wife or watching cartoons with his children.

Glossary

Apothecary: a person who prepared and sold medicines and drugs.

Arbalist: a person who shoots a crossbow. A crossbowman.

Baldric: a belt for a sword or other piece of equipment, worn over one shoulder and reaching down to the opposite hip.

Barrow: a mound of earth and stones raised over a grave or graves. A burial mound.

Beryl: a pale green or blue. The color is derived from the mineral with the same name.

Carrion: the decaying flesh of dead animals. Carcasses.

Cinnabar: a bright scarlet to brick red form of mercury ore. It is the source of the brilliant red or scarlet pigment named vermillion.

Codex: an ancient manuscript text in book form.

Corvus: a genus of birds which includes species such as crows, ravens, rooks, and jackdaws.

Darkstone: a matte black orb that may be a type of stone. When exposed to blood, the sphere extrudes a gray mineral that is highly coveted for its properties. Bearers of the stones experience nightmares and visions of a dark figure.

Dell: a small valley, usually among trees.

Fiefdom: a noble's sphere of operation or control. A fief. An estate of land.

Flora: the plants of a particular region, habitat, or geological period.

Fullers: a rounded or beveled groove or slot along the flat side of a blade.

Hearth: the floor of a fireplace.

Herald: a messenger bringing news.

Hypogeum: an underground chamber.

Immolating: death by burning.

Millennia: many thousands of years.

Narrow leafed campion: a species of flowering plant that was resurrected from a 32,000 year old biological sample by a team of scientists in 2012.

Onyx: a variety of agate, often black.

Oxide: a black coating used as a protective or decorative layer over metal.

Parapet: a low protective wall along the edge of a roof, bridge, or balcony.

Pauldron: a component of plate armor that covers the shoulder.

Peregrine: a falcon and bird of prey, renowned for being the fastest member of the animal kingdom.

Pommel: the end of the handle of a sword, dagger, or old-fashioned gun. They are usually round or blunt.

Psilocybin: a type of mushroom that produces a psychedelic drug compound.

Quarry: to extract stone or other materials from a place, typically a large, deep pit.

Rock dove: a common pigeon.

Rouge: a red powder or cream used as a cosmetic for coloring the cheeks or lips.

Sable: a black color.

Sanguine: blood red.

Scabbard: a sheath for the blade of a sword or dagger, typically made of leather or metal.

Scrivening: writing.

Spire: a tapering structure at the top of a building, like a tower.

Standard: an emblem that is either a flag or rigid mobile image, which is used as a formal, visual symbol of a state, prince, military unit, etc.

Viscous: having a thick, sticky consistency between solid and liquid.

Wraith: a ghost or ghostlike image of a person.

Zealot: someone who is fanatical and uncompromising.

Made in the USA
Coppell, TX
16 June 2020